WE BELONG

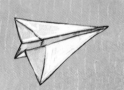

LAURA PURDIE SALAS

ILLUSTRATED BY CARLOS VÉLEZ AGUILERA

Carolrhoda Books
Minneapolis

FOR MY FRIEND LISA BULLARD, WHO HELPS PEOPLE KNOW THEY BELONG
—L.P.S.

TO MY FATHER AND MOTHER, WHO MADE MY WORLD A BEAUTIFUL PLACE TO BELONG
—C.V.A.

Carolrhoda Books®
An imprint of Lerner Publishing Group, Inc.
241 First Avenue North
Minneapolis, MN 55401 USA

For reading levels and more information, look up this title at www.lernerbooks.com.

Designed by Lindsey Owens.
Main body text set in Tw Cen MT Std.
Typeface provided by Monotype Typography.
The illustrations in this book were created with colored pencil and digital media.

Library of Congress Cataloging-in-Publication Data

Names: Salas, Laura Purdie, author. | Vélez, Carlos, 1980- illustrator.
Title: We belong / Laura Purdie Salas ; illustrated by Carlos Vélez Aguilera.
Description: Minneapolis, MN : Carolrhoda Books, [2021] | Audience: Ages 4–8. | Audience: Grades K–1. | Summary: Whether tall or short or weak or strong, we all have value and we all belong.
Identifiers: LCCN 2021028585 (print) | LCCN 2021028586 (ebook) | ISBN 9781541599130 | ISBN 9781728443911 (ebook)
Subjects: CYAC: Stories in rhyme. | Opposites—Fiction. | LCGFT: Picture books.
Classification: LCC PZ8.3.S166 We 2021 (print) | LCC PZ8.3.S166 (ebook) | DDC [E]—dc23

LC record available at https://lccn.loc.gov/2021028585
LC ebook record available at https://lccn.loc.gov/2021028586

Manufactured in the United States of America
1-48109-48762-7/14/2021

There are so many excellent things we can do,

and I'm glad we are here.
I'm glad that you're you.

Maybe you're quiet.

You wonder.

You dream.

Thoughts trickle softly, clear as a stream.

Maybe you're loud.

**AH-CHOOOOOO!
RAT-A-TAT!**

Nobody says, "Can you repeat that?"

Quiet and loud both deserve our applause.
What makes music sing is the sound
and . . .

the pause.

Fireworks grab us with
BANG!
BOOM!
POP!
And the soft, smoky sizzle
when the big noises stop.

Maybe you're tall as a big redwood tree.
When your kite becomes stuck, you just pluck it free!
From the very back row, you can still see the screen.

On the basketball court,
you're a slam-dunk machine!

Maybe you're short.
Down low to the ground.
Constantly turning the lost into found.
In hide-and-seek games, you can barely be seen.

On class party day,
you're a limbo machine!

Does it matter?
And why?

We're each only as high as a small grain of sand next to mountains or sky.

Maybe you're happy.
A fun magic trick.

A sprinkler rainbow.
A kitten's rough lick.

Maybe you're sad.
A cloud.
A small cave.

Maybe you're trying
your best to be brave.

Sometimes we'd like to make sadness extinct,

but teardrops and smiles are joined—
they are linked.

Each feeling's a gift
that helps us connect
to the world,
to our family,
to the friends we collect.

Does the world call you Black?
Does it say you are white?
Whatever its color, your skin is just right.

We all wear our skin just like trees wear their bark,
in infinite shades between light and dark.

Are you river birch?

Hazelnut?

Chestnut or cherry?

Jack pine?

Mahogany?

Oak or mulberry?

Let's all show the world what we carry within,

our lifelong journey,
the places we've been,

the family we love,
   the dreams that we dream,
      and the people we are deep inside of our skin.

There are boys. There are girls.
And even more choices.
Let's build a world where there's room for all voices.

Play with the toys that you think are fun.
Put on a tutu and hit a home run!
Be who you feel like.
CHOOSE WHO YOU ARE.

Let your own heart be your guiding North Star.

Maybe you're local,
born here, in this town.
Know the trees to climb up
and the slides to slide down.

When you are the expert on the place where you live—
what a cheerful and friendly welcome you'll give!

Do you come from close by?

From a town that's quite near?

The one with tall buildings and the old, wooden pier?

Or maybe you come from some other land.
Did you drive along highways? Trek across sand?
Did you have a front yard or a field full of sheep?
Did traffic or sirens keep you from sleep?

If we could stand on the moon,
we'd see earth—round and small . . .
one dazzling, spinning, blue-and-green ball,
one circular swirl that is home to us all.

When we learn from each other,
we expand what we know.

Our hearts crack open,
like seeds,
and they grow.

You and I, we're alike,
but we're different too.

That's not good.
That's not bad.

It's just what is true.

And here,
in this space—

THIS IS WHERE WE BELONG.